Beautiful Junk

Beautiful Junk

A Story of the Watts Towers

by Jon Madian

With Photographs by
Barbara and Lou Jacobs, Jr.

Little, Brown and Company
Boston   Toronto

Published simultaneously in Canada
by Little, Brown & Company (Canada) Limited

PRINTED IN THE UNITED STATES OF AMERICA

For Gisele and Lori

Charlie didn't notice the sun setting behind the telephone lines. The alley was already dark with the shadows of evening. Charlie sat near some trash cans. He raised a steel pipe above his head.

"Junk, dirty junk!" he said angrily. And he smashed the bottle lying on the pavement before him. The glass shattered into a hundred pieces.

Charlie went over to the trash can and found another bottle. He put it on the pavement. "Junk, junk, dirty junk!" he shouted as he hit it with the pipe. Then he beat the pavement harder and yelled louder, "Junk! Junk! Dirty, dirty junk!"

Charlie was so busy beating and shouting that he didn't see the old man come around the corner. He was pushing a wheelbarrow full of empty bottles, rusted wire, and other things collected from the back alleys.

The old man put down the wheelbarrow and watched. When Charlie was tired of banging, he looked up. He was surprised and a little frightened too. The old man was looking right at him.

"What do you want?" asked Charlie.

"Some bottles and wire," said the old man in a quiet voice. "But I see you've broken all the bottles. Did you see any wire in the trash cans?"

"Why do you want bottles and wire?" asked Charlie. "Do you get money for 'em?"

"No," answered the old man.

Then he bent over and looked at the broken pieces of glass at Charlie's feet.

"May I have some of these?" he asked.

"You want that junk?" asked Charlie in disbelief. "Sure, take it."

The old man picked out special pieces of glass. Then he took a brown bag from his pocket, unfolded it, and carefully placed the pieces of glass inside.

"Man, who ever heard of collectin' busted-up glass," said Charlie.

"Some of these pieces are beautiful. You broke them into fine shapes."

"Beautiful!" exclaimed Charlie with a laugh. "You must be blind. That glass is junk. Ugly junk, like everything in this alley, and everything in your wheelbarrow."

The old man looked at his wheelbarrow, then he looked at Charlie.

"Maybe you're right," he said. He bent over
the wheelbarrow and pushed it down the shadowy
alley.

A few days later, as Charlie left school with his friend Sammy, he saw the old man across the street. His wheelbarrow was heaped full of broken dishes and rusted pipes, and tied on the top was a metal gate.

Charlie pointed at the old man and said, "He thinks broken glass is beautiful." Then he cupped his hands to his mouth and shouted. "Look at the beautiful junk! Look at the beautiful junk!"

The boys laughed.

Charlie did not see the old man again for many weeks, and he had almost forgotten about him.

Then one evening he and Sammy were playing in a vacant lot. They had found some old records which someone had thrown away. They tied the records to a string and shot at them with their slingshots.

Just as they were taking aim at a record, the old man came around the corner. The boys spoke loudly. "Now look at that beautiful record!" They both opened fire. The rocks whizzed through the air and smashed the record to pieces.

"You're good shots," said the old man.

"We like to break records," said Charlie.

"I hope you won't break them all."

"Why not?" asked Sammy. "They're no good to no one. They're scratched."

"Because . . ." began the old man.

" 'Cause he thinks they're beautiful," interrupted Charlie.

"I think so. I can use them even if they're scratched."

"What's pretty 'bout a black record?" demanded Charlie.

"Its shape is perfect," said the old man. "Can you think of anything else that has so many perfect circles, one right next to the other?"

After a moment, Charlie said, "I bet you want a record."

"I would use it if you gave it to me."

Charlie handed him a record, and the old man went on his way down the alley.

"He's a crazy man!" exclaimed Sammy, looking after him.

"I wonder where he takes all that junk," said Charlie.

"Search me," said Sammy.

And the boys tied another record to the string and gathered some more stones.

"The old man must be crazy," thought Charlie as he lay in bed that night. "But tomorrow I'll follow him and see what he does with all that junk."

After school, Charlie and Sammy played in the vacant lot, but the old man did not come by. All that week and the first part of the next week, Charlie searched the streets near his home.

Finally, Wednesday, while eating lunch with Sammy, Charlie saw the old man pushing his empty wheelbarrow outside the school fence.

"There he is!" Charlie shouted. "Let's follow him!"

"We can't take off now," said Sammy. "We got to stay in school."

"I'm not stayin'. Come on, now's our chance!" exclaimed Charlie.

"And get picked up by that truant guy for cuttin'," answered Sammy.

"Okay, if you're scared, I'll follow him myself,"
said Charlie, and he climbed the fence and started
after the old man.

Charlie stayed a good distance behind so he would not be seen. The old man turned down an alley. Carefully, he looked through the things in a trash can. He chose a bottle, held it up to the sun, spun it around, laughed, and placed it in his wheelbarrow.

The school bell rang in the distance. Suddenly it was quiet in the alley. "What if the truant officer finds me?" Charlie thought. "What will they do to me at school?" He wished that Sammy were with him.

The old man looked in another trash can and found some pieces of broken tile. At still another trash can he picked out a cookie cutter shaped like a heart. And so it went. For two hours Charlie followed the old man as he collected dozens of discarded pieces of once-useful things from the trash cans.

Charlie had never been in so many alleys before, or so far from home.

At last the wheelbarrow was full. The old man started off without stopping to check any more trash cans. He walked more quickly, humming as he went.

Charlie was surprised at how fast the old man could walk. And he didn't know why anyone pushing such a load of junk would be singing . . . unless, maybe Sammy was right. Maybe the old man was really crazy.

Down one street, around a corner, down another street, through traffic, across railroad tracks, Charlie followed the old man. He was in a neighborhood he had never seen before. A police car went by, and again he thought of the truant officer.

The old man disappeared around a corner. Charlie ran to be sure not to lose sight of him. He rushed around the corner — and crash! He ran right into the old man's wheelbarrow. It tipped over with a bang. Junk flew everywhere, and Charlie fell to the sidewalk.

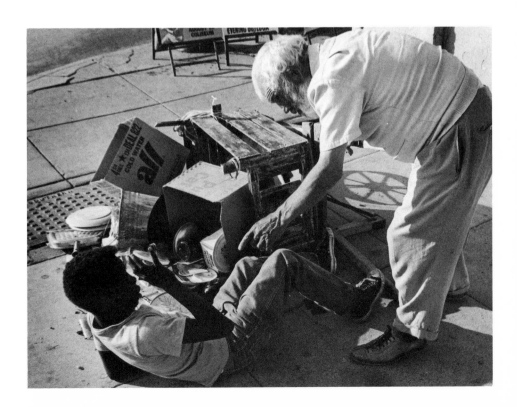

"Why have you followed me?" asked the old man, looking down at Charlie, and waving his hand angrily.

"I . . . I didn't. You can't prove it," stammered Charlie as he got back to his feet.

"All right," said the old man as he bent over and began reloading the wheelbarrow. "I just thought that you were following me. I wondered why."

Charlie could see that the old man wasn't going to hurt him, so he confessed, "I want to see where you take the junk you collect."

"Oh, I can't let you find that out," said the old man. "You might come and break my things."

"I don't care anyway," answered Charlie, but he really did care.

The old man was silent for a long time while he reloaded the wheelbarrow. Then he asked, "If I show you, will you promise never to come and break any of my things?"

"I promise," said Charlie.

The old man turned around, bent over, took the handles of the wheelbarrow in his strong hands, and began to walk and hum. Charlie followed a few steps behind.

They went a few more blocks and came to some railroad tracks. They crossed the tracks and then Charlie saw, rising high in the air, three tall pointed towers. He had never seen anything like them before. They looked like some queer kind of fairy-tale towers.

The old man pushed his wheelbarrow along the wall which enclosed the towers. He unlocked a gate, and went in. Charlie followed, his heart beating fast with excitement.

Everywhere Charlie looked, there were strange
structures made of cement and decorated with
hundreds of broken pieces of glass, old tiles,
bottles, and shells. And the cement itself had
many designs cut into it. There were designs made
by cookie cutters and by records and many other
things which Charlie recognized. It was like a
magic land. So many colors and circles and arches

and shapes, and high above them all were the three
tall towers.

"Do you see the junk?" the old man asked as he
began unloading the wheelbarrow. "This is where
I bring it."

"Here?" asked Charlie in disbelief. "You bring
it here?"

"Yes, I use it to build, to build the towers and

all the things you see. I'm a poor man. I can't buy things to build with. So I build with things from trash cans, vacant lots, and junkyards. Things people think are no good. I have made those things into something beautiful.''

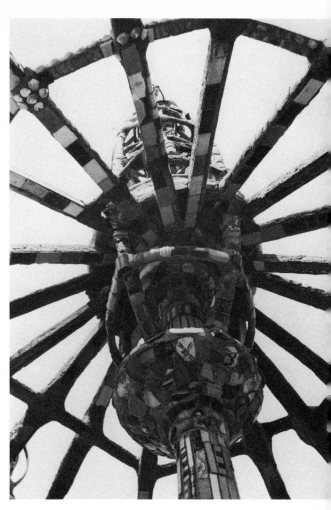

Charlie gazed about for a long time without
saying anything. He didn't know what he ex-
pected when he followed the old man, but he cer-
tainly didn't expect this.

The old man's eyes sparkled when he saw how
excited Charlie was.

"You can go look around," he said, "but re-
member your promise."
Charlie nodded and started off to explore.

The old man mixed some water, sand, and cement in a large bucket. He carried the bucket of cement, some broken tiles, and some bottle ends over to a corner. He smeared the wet cement on the wall. Then he pressed the bits of broken tile into the wet cement. Charlie came over. He watched the old man making a flowerlike design.

"Would you hand me those bottle ends?" asked the old man. "I'll put them here next to the tile."

Charlie handed him the bottle ends. He liked the flower the old man was making.

"Did you make all of this yourself?" he asked.

"All of it," said the old man. "I put in every stone, tile, bottle, shell, design, and shape . . . everything."

"Man!" declared Charlie. "You musta worked a long time."

"More than thirty years," said the old man, and he smeared more fresh cement on the wall.

"How did you build those high towers?" asked Charlie.

"I made them strong with metal, wire, and cement. I climbed up, building them as I climbed. Sometimes I took my lunch up with me."

"Can I climb them?" asked Charlie excitedly.

"Go ahead, but be careful," warned the old man.

So Charlie began to climb the highest tower. He wanted to go to the very top. But when he was about halfway up, he looked down. The ground was far below him. The old man looked very small. Charlie waved down at him, and he didn't climb any higher.

After Charlie climbed back down, he asked, "When you're finished, will you sell it?"

The old man laughed. "No, no, I didn't build this to sell."

"Then why'd you build it?" asked Charlie.

"Because," began the old man. Then he paused. Slowly he looked all about him, at all the wonderful things he had made. "Because I wanted to build something beautiful."

Charlie wasn't sure he understood why someone would work for so long just to build something beautiful. But he was sure that he liked what the old man had built.

"Can I play here again?" he asked.

The old man smiled. "I'd like that."

"And maybe I could help you," said Charlie. "After school tomorrow, I'll bring some things from my alley."

The old man looked at an empty spot along the wall.

"Maybe we can build a wishing well over there," he said. "I thought I was almost finished, but with a strong boy like you to help me, I can build some more."

"How does a wishing well look?" asked Charlie.

"Like we want it to. Bring your beautiful junk tomorrow, Charlie, and we'll build it together."

Postscript

The towers which Charlie discovered in the story actually exist. They can be seen in the Watts section of Los Angeles, California, where they were built by an old man named Simon Rodia.

Simon Rodia was a poor man who worked as a tile setter. He liked to read about heroes like Marco Polo, Columbus, and Galileo. Once he said that a person has to do "good good or bad bad to be remembered." Maybe it was because Simon Rodia wanted to be remembered for doing something very good that he worked for thirty-three years to build the towers.

Simon Rodia worked all alone. He used only the simple tools of a tile setter and a window washer's belt and bucket. For building materials, he collected more than seventy-thousand seashells, dismantled pipe structures and steel bedframes, and salvaged countless tiles and bottles.

In 1954, at the age of seventy-five, Simon Rodia completed his work, and he moved away. Many people thought he was a crazy man for building the towers. Children broke the tile and glass decorations. In 1957, Simon Rodia's house burned down. It seemed that his work was going to be destroyed and forgotten.

Some people realized how wonderful the towers were and wanted to save them. But the Los Angeles City Building Department said that the towers must be detroyed because they were unsafe, having been built from junk and with inferior construction methods.

A missile test engineer, using space-age calculations, showed that though Simon Rodia had little book knowledge of the right way to build, his construction was safe. The building officials still were not satisfied. A pull test of the tallest tower was ordered. A cable was hooked from a truck to the top of the tallest tower. While television cameras turned and hundreds of people watched, the truck strained to pull the tower down. A shout of joy went up from the crowd. The tower stood firm. Only one seashell had fallen out of place.

Today people come from all over the world to enjoy Simon Rodia's towers. Pictures of the towers appear in magazines from Tokyo to Paris. Simon Rodia's dream has come true. He is remembered for something beautiful.